CRUISING FOR LOVE

A SHORT STORY VACATION ROMANCE

MELANIE A. SMITH

BOOKS BY MELANIE A. SMITH

The Safeguarded Heart Series

The Safeguarded Heart

All of Me

Never Forget

Her Dirty Secret

Recipes from the Heart: A Companion to the Safeguarded Heart Series

The Safeguarded Heart Complete Series: All Five Books and Exclusive Bonus Material

Life Lessons: A series that can be read as standalones

Never Date a Doctor

Bad Boys Don't Make Good Boyfriends

You Can't Buy Love

The Heart of Rutherford: Life Lessons Novels 1 – 3

Standalone Romance Novels

Everybody Lies

Last Kiss Under the Mistletoe

Tough Love

Finding His Redemption

Short Stories

Cruising for Love

Hot for Santa

Anthologies

Heroes With Heat and Heart 2: A Charity Anthology

CRUISING FOR LOVE

This is it. This is how I'm going to die.

Lost on a fucking cruise ship before I even get to my cabin, I'm going to be snatched by the Russian mob, sold into sex slavery, then killed by some rapist sleazebag.

Okay, maybe I'm being a touch *paranoid*, I decide as I realize the room numbers are climbing away from my assigned suite. With a sigh, I turn around and start heading back down the never-ending hallway, hooking a left and praying I'll run into someone helpful and not, you know, someone who will kidnap me.

It's all Kevin McDonald's fault, really. If the motherfucker hadn't been cheating on me with his goddamn secretary, of all the clichés, I wouldn't have had to end our engagement and go on this cruise alone. Because

I'll be damned if I'm wasting piles of money because of that bastard. That's right, I paid for the damn trip, sucker that I am. So alone or not, I'm going to enjoy these two weeks to their fullest. And then some. With or without a safety net. Pun. Intended.

In the smallest of favors granted by a universe that hasn't been kind to me lately, while I don't run into anyone helpful, I do somehow manage to stumble upon my room. I let out a triumphant yelp and slide my card through the door's reader. But when I step into the small space, my excitement dissolves faster than my three-year relationship did when I found naked pictures of Sandra on Kevin's phone.

Because the damn bed is covered with rose petals. A chilled bottle of Champagne sits in a bucket at the end of the bed. There are candles everywhere flicking dimly. They're obviously the fake LED kind, but they still give the room a decidedly romantic feel.

I purse my lips. Nuh uh.

I promptly retreat back into the hallway, leaving my luggage behind. And then I go in search of booze. Lots and lots of booze.

Good thing I got the drink package, is my first thought.

My second thought makes me snicker. *Two*. I have *two* drink packages. It might just be enough to make me

not care about the romantic setting when I come back
to the cabin to pass out.

THE INSTANT MY EYES LAND ON HIM, MY SLOPPY
three-drinks-down ass knows. This is the guy I'm going
to have crazy sex with all over those goddamn rose
petals in a grand display of Fuck-You-Kevin.

I snort loudly at the thought and then self-
consciously glance around. Thankfully nobody in the
loud bar seemed to notice the un-lady-like slovenly pig
noise. On some level, I recognize I may already be too
tipsy to make this decision. But … if I can even question that, I'm not *that* far gone, right?

So while I'm still confident I can walk in a straight
line and not slur my words, I plunk my glass down,
rise, and let the liquid courage propel me across the
packed room to Mister Right-Now.

I'd picked him because of the broad back that was
faced toward me, clearly well-muscled and flowing into
a trim waist, that in turn leads to the tightest, most
gorgeous ass I've seen in a long time. It only gets better
the closer I get, the denim seemingly molded to fit the
perfection that is this man's backside.

I manage to tear my eyes away long enough to

notice that the guy he's chatting with has spotted me and is leaning in to whisper to my target, causing Mr. Nice Ass to turn around.

My heart practically leaps out of my chest as electric-blue eyes meet mine. I stop a few feet away, literally focusing all my energy on not swooning. *Swooning.* I don't fucking swoon. Oh boy. This guy is trouble.

A cat-like grin spreads over my face.

I'm definitely in the mood for some trouble.

The guy's mouth quirks in an answering mischievous smile as his eyes slowly trail down my body. He must approve of the breezy, strapless flower-print number that hits mid-thigh, because his eyes meet mine again and he cocks his head invitingly.

As if they have a mind of their own, my legs start moving, propelling me toward him. And as I stop next to him, I have to crane my head to look up. He's nearly a foot taller than my five-feet-three-inches. Oof.

"Hi, I'm Dakota," I find myself saying, sticking my hand out. Then I'm immediately fighting the urge not to face-palm. *'Hi, I'm Dakota'? Really? Laaaaaame.*

But Nice Ass doesn't seem to mind, his much larger hand closing over mine.

"I'm Kade."

The deep voice sends tingles down my spine and

drains all thought from my brain. I stand there, dumbly shaking his hand and staring into his eyes as he stares back, the air between us thick with tension.

"And I'm Rob," his friend pipes up sarcastically. "Not that it matters."

I huff indistinctly, meaning to apologize and meet the guy's eye … but I can't seem to tear my gaze from Kade's. After a moment, Rob huffs a laugh and walks away. Kade doesn't seem to notice or care.

"Can I buy you a drink, Dakota?" he finally asks.

His hand slips from mine and it gives me the strength to break eye contact, my eyes moving to the massive chest straining against the dark T-shirt he's wearing. I lick my lips and look back up at him.

"What?" I ask dumbly. My mind was so involved in wondering what he looks like under that shirt I completely forgot what he just asked.

A low chuckle meets my ears and my eyes bounce back up to his. But he's leaned down into my space and he's much, much closer than I expected him to be. His lips inches from mine, my whole body tenses in the most delicious way.

"Or maybe you just want to get out of here?" he asks quietly.

Oof again. I think I'm going to have to, if for nothing else than to get out of these wet panties. The man hasn't spoken twenty words to me or even touched me yet and I'm ready for this. And the internal voice that would normally warn me off such a skeevy-seeming invitation has been silenced by the sheer attraction between us, by the hurt still roiling in my heart, and by the liquid courage zipping through my veins.

I've never had a one-night stand. Never had sex with someone whose name I just barely learned. And yet…

I nod. Unable to bring myself to care whether this is an epically awful decision.

His lip pulls up on one side, and I feel his hand slide over mine again. But my eyes are still locked on his as if in a trance.

I feel him lift my hand to his mouth. I watch him place a kiss on the back, his lips softly caressing the skin. He leans down even closer, hovering beside my neck. His hot breath on the shell of my ear awakens every nerve in my body. He smells like a mix of expensive aftershave and … Band-Aids? The recognition jars me out of my daze just a little … that is, until his voice drags me back under.

"Your cabin or mine?" he asks huskily.

My skin flushes equally from embarrassment and anticipation.

But I'm not going to be a shrinking flower here. I want this.

"Mine," I say firmly, clamping down on his hand and pulling him toward the door.

As soon as we're in the hallway, Kade yanks on my hand, spinning me around, and pushes me up against the wall. The breath leaves my body as I prepare to be jumped on … but his prowl is slow, deliberate. Even hotter than being shoved up against a wall and kissed stupid.

He cages me in. Runs the back of his hand down my cheek. Drops his face almost lazily to mine.

I stare up at him, entranced. Yes. This is definitely hotter than hot, I decide as his lips settle over mine tentatively.

My response is anything but tentative. I push into him, sliding my hands up his chest as I open my mouth to him. God, his chest is so hard. His shoulders so damn wide. He feels like stone under my hands as he truly claims my mouth this time.

His tongue dances along my lip before dipping into my mouth, sending me spinning. His hands likewise dip to my ass, pulling me against his rock-hard core, and I swear I almost come just feeling how huge and hard he is against my center.

Yes. This is exactly what I need. To wipe that

cheating bastard from my mind and body with a complete stranger. Not knowing anything about him is definitely landing this in full-on fantasy territory, and I'm here for it.

I let my hands slide over his back. Holy hell. I have got to see all these muscles. Now.

I break my mouth away, and through the panting, manage, "It's not far." I give a vague gesture in the direction of my room.

His lip curls into that sensual smile of his and he steps back, allowing me to continue pulling him along.

And lordy if I can't go fast enough. My girly parts are definitely running the show now, because this time I find my room without any trouble at all. Who knew my vagina had such a good sense of direction? Straight toward the fastest route to get an unbelievably gorgeous guy between my thighs, apparently.

I let Kade in and close the door behind us, leaning back against the contoured plastic. He looks at the setup on the bed then looks over at me, one eyebrow cocked.

"Had plans, did you?" His tone is teasing, light. His dark hair looks inky-black in the dim light, soft tendrils brushing the tops of his ears and his forehead. The contrast against the hard planes of his face truly high-lights just how striking he is.

I shake my head. "Had. Now I have new plans. Ones that don't involve a lot of talking."

He assesses me for a moment, almost like he gets what I'm not saying. But he doesn't comment, instead stalking deliberately toward me.

"Oh there will be talking," he declares confidently, caging me against the door. His thumb strokes my arm as his mouth leans in to graze my neck. "Dirty talk." He kisses my collarbone. "Telling me how you want it." I arch into him as his lips move upward. "Screaming my name." I draw in a sharp breath and he suckles the spot under my ear. I feel him smile against my skin.

I swallow hard and lick my lips. "I like your plan better," I admit.

He chuckles and tugs at a curly blond lock that escaped my ponytail before pulling me by the waist toward the bed.

He picks up the Champagne bucket and presses me down onto the bed in its place.

"And we're definitely going to enjoy this." He sets the bucket on the dresser opposite the end of the bed. "But first …"

And my heart stops when he whips his shirt off.

Oh. My. God.

The man is *cut*. Massive taut pecs over a god. Damn. Eight. Pack. Not to mention that sharp cut V that leads to the top of his pants. You know, the one that makes smart girls dumb. And as smart as I normally am, that's how dumb I've gone for this Adonis.

I'm suddenly on board with the Champagne idea, so long as I get to drink it out of the deep grooves surrounding his muscles.

I stand without thinking, turning him around and pushing him onto the bed, my urgency clear in my quick movements. Without fanfare, I kick off my kitten-heeled sandals, pull my sundress over my head, then loose my long locks from the hairband. I don't even give Kade time to take in my nude bra and barely-there thong before climbing on top of him.

My lips and hips work against his, and in no time his rough hands are grabbing my ass. I grind into his impressive erection, needing the friction. Needing that feeling that will replace everything else.

I'm just getting tingles started low in my belly when Kade flips us on the bed and pulls away. He laughs at the confused, butt-hurt look I surely must have on my face.

"Trust me." He winks, and I bite my lip at how sexy he is. "Damn, Dakota, you are *beautiful*." He draws out the word on a breath. And in any other circumstances that would make me roll my eyes, but instead it makes me feel exactly that way under his hot gaze. Beautiful.

And bold. I prop myself up and unhook my bra, dropping it over the side of the bed while I hold Kade's gaze. His eyes widen, but don't leave mine. With a grin, I reach down and wiggle out of my panties, holding them up for him to see and letting them fall on top of my bra.

Suddenly, he's yanking my feet toward him, sliding my ass to the end of the bed. He drops so fast I barely mark the motion before I feel his mouth between my legs. His tongue wasting no time flicking against my clit, his fingers plunging mercilessly into me. I cry out and bow off the bed.

"Take it, Dakota," he hums between my legs. "Take it all, beautiful. You taste like fucking heaven."

His hand presses against my pelvis, keeping me in place for his feast. Letting there be no escape from the sudden, intense pleasure.

And my god, the pleasure. White hot fire spreads through my lower abdomen, swirling and tightening as his skilled ministrations hurtle me toward orgasm.

I look down at him, desperate for release. The intensity of his eyes almost pushes me over the edge. I bite into my lip so hard I'm afraid I may draw blood. But I just can't take it anymore.

"Please," I whimper.

Kade's teeth graze my clit. "You ready to come?"

I nod. His tongue laps once at the tight bud.

"You gonna come so hard for me, Dakota?"

I clench and groan. "God, yes, please," I beg.

"Good girl. Come for me now." His tongue and fingers work in a frenzy. So crazy fast that the release hits like a lightning bolt, splitting me in half. Sweet death by ecstasy.

He pulls away and I'm left panting and half-blind with the aftermath of my release. But I can hear slushy ice moving. A cork popping. And then he's on top of me, his mouth pressing against mine.

My hands find his face as cold sparkling wine slips through my lips. I accept the drink, gulping greedily so I can free my mouth to do other things. Our tongues tangle as he settles between my legs. I feel the fabric of his jeans against me and decide that just won't do.

I press at his chest and he pulls back enough for me to reach between us and pop the button on his pants. A deep groan rumbles through his chest as I slip my hand in to find him without underwear, hard as granite, and silky soft to the touch.

"Fuck." The curse slips through my lips as my hand gets a good feel for his length. I scooch forward until I'm on the end of the bed, then push his hips back so I can shimmy his jeans off. He obliges, kicking them off his feet. So vigorously that he falls onto the bed, laughing.

"I'm at your mercy," he says with a chuckle.

With a grin, I snatch the opened bottle of bubbly from behind me and climb over him.

"Good. Because it's time for revenge," I promise, taking a few deep gulps before saving a mouthful for him. I give it to him the same way he'd done before pulling away. And then I pour some over his chest and abs.

He laughs in shock. "Don't waste it!"

I flex a brow. "Oh, I won't." And I proceed to lick my way down his chest, getting every last drop before taking his huge cock into my mouth. His laughter turns to a deep groan of pleasure that brings back the wetness between my legs.

"Damn, that's good," he moans.

I lick around the crown so I can smile up at him, all while continuing to pump his shaft.

"Yes, just like that," he encourages me.

I spin my hand and squeeze as I move it up and down and he throws his head back. "Tell me what you want," I say, turning the tables. Taking us to part two of his plan.

His head snaps up and he smirks. "You're a naughty one," he hums.

I drop his cock and hover over it so my chest is barely grazing him. "That wasn't an answer."

His eyes darken and he sits up. I scramble back instinctively at the ferociousness in his expression. "I want to fuck another three orgasms out of you, Dakota. I want to feel your pussy wet and dripping just for me. I want to make you come so hard, and so loud, that you forget everything but the feeling of my dick inside you."

My eyes go wide but I have little time to respond as he plows me over onto my back, his hard length pressed into my leg as he grabs for a strip of condoms he somehow placed on the nightstand. Seconds later, a rip of foil, a swift roll down his length, and his hand is between my legs, priming me.

"Now, tell me what *you* want," he says in a low voice that is full of carnal promise.

"Everything," I breathe tensely. He gives me a look of exasperation that makes me smile. "I want you on top of me. Behind me. Next to me. I want to be on top of you. I want it deep and hard. And slow and soft. I want you to smack my ass and bite my nipples then pull my hair. I want you to make love to me. I want you to do whatever dirty thing you want to me."

I watch his cock jump at every sentence, but when I'm done his face is hard as stone.

"That all?" he asks drily.

I grin. "It'll do for a start."

The first real grin I've seen from him breaks over his face, and he's so angelically beautiful it hurts.

"Well. We'd best get started then."

He fists himself up and down as I watch. Wondering what he'll do next.

He continues his stroking, holding my gaze and leaning down. His mouth covers my core, his tongue licking up my pussy. I clench but don't break eye contact. I want to watch.

And watch I do, as he seats himself at my entrance. As he slowly pushes in. As he watches me back. Heat spreads over my cheeks as the sensation of him filling me, painful and sweet, sends ripples through my body. Once he's in to the hilt, he moves slowly. My hips tilt and twist with need.

With a small smile, he presses my knees toward my chest and goes in deeper. "You like that?" he asks, pushing in.

"Yes. More," I demand.

He presses my knees as far back as they'll go and sinks all the way in. We both groan at the intense, tight fit.

"Now, f—"

But before I can finish giving the order, he's

pounding me so hard another orgasm shatters through me in seconds. He pulls out while I'm still quivering, flips me over, then slides back in and continues slamming into me. It's beyond intense, beyond words, beyond screaming. I sink against the mattress as my pussy quivers with the dregs of my last orgasm and the beginning of my next.

"No relaxing on my watch," Kade teases, pressing fully into me while he gathers my hair. I feel him wrap it around a fist and tug.

Just when I didn't think it could get better.

I bow upward, allowing him to pull me taut by my hair. Once he has me locked in place, he resumes, his thrusts hard but slow.

"Touch yourself," he commands gruffly. I arch deeper at his words, and he pulls tighter.

I clamp a hand roughly over one nipple and the other drops to my clit. I pull hard at my breast while pressing rough circles between my legs in the same rhythm Kade is taking me.

"Fuck, I'm gonna … I'm gonna …" I pant.

Kade speeds up and flexes his pelvis to tilt deep and hard every time he hits home. His balls slapping my ass. His grunts filling my ears. I glance back to see every muscle in his glorious body flexing as he works to bring me to orgasm and it drives me out of my mind with pleasure. I hit my peak and stay there by greedily rubbing myself on his cock. He allows it, encourages it, fucks me through every last moment of my lengthy orgasm, then slowly lowers me to the bed. I sink into the mattress, bliss heating my veins, my nipples and clit throbbing with pain that feels so good.

He slides behind me. "No rest for the wicked, lover," he murmurs in my ear. And I feel his hot, hard cock nudging between my thighs. I lean back into him with a smile and lift my leg to rest over his. He slides into me from behind, but oh-so-gently. "Feel okay?"

His curved cock has nestled itself perfectly in me, gently rubbing over that spot inside.

"Feels fantastic," I murmur. "Don't stop."

Kade's mouth presses into my shoulder blade while one hand reaches under my rib cage to reach up and circle my nipple, the other holding my pelvis at just such an angle so he can pump into me in long, slow strokes that feel like heaven. While I know already I won't reach orgasm this way, the build is so slow and so luxurious, I can't say I mind.

Eventually, it seem Kade realizes he won't get there this way either. "I want you on top of me, Dakota," he murmurs against my skin.

I flex my hips forward so he pops out, and I roll away. Taking the opportunity for a small break, I stand up and get another drink of Champagne. The cold liquid sliding down my throat is refreshing and invigorating. I turn and offer the bottle to Kade.

With what seems to be his trademark smirk, he props himself up and takes it. I climb onto his lap as he drinks, then he hands the bottle back to me. I take a long drink, leaving the last sip for him.

He laughs and shakes his head. "I like your style." He finishes the bottle and chucks it onto the floor all while maintaining some seriously sexy eye contact. And I need no other invitation.

His hand slips around my back as I rise to settle over him. His other hand positions his cock to spear me. And I sink back down into bliss.

I bounce gently on him, my tits teasing his chin. His mouth finds one as he flexes his hips in time to my rhythm. This time the build isn't slow or fast. It's natural. The perfectly paced climb to enjoy every sensation without racing to the finish.

Kade's mouth stops worshipping my nipples long enough to meet mine in a brief, intense kiss. "You're amazing, Dakota."

"You feel so good, Kade," I reply, rolling my hips over his and moaning. "You are so good."

"It's easy to be when you're so fucking sexy," he

responds. His hand drifts down to my clit. "Especially when you're coming."

My brows pinch together as what he's doing to me winds the coil inside tighter. God, he knows exactly what buttons to push and when to make me come. And I can't say I mind.

My hips grind harder, faster, chasing the high I know is about to hit. I tip my head back and close my eyes.

"Say my name, Dakota," he whispers.

I tighten around him and he inhales sharply.

"God, Kade," I moan. He bucks into me. "Oh, Kade, yes." His movements become as desperate as mine and it's fast and hard and all friction and …. "Kade, oh god, yes, Kade, there, there, Kade…"

"Dakota, fuck, yes," Kade grinds out as he thickens inside me, his hands tightening around my waist and pulling me fully and sharply onto his final thrust.

I float down from my peak and rest my forehead against his. We breathe in each other's scents. We smell like sweat, and pussy, and come, and fucking nirvana. My brain is buzzing on a level that makes full thoughts impossible.

It's glorious.

I feel Kade roll me gently onto the bed and withdraw. I don't realize my eyes are closed until I feel his weight sink back on the bed next to me. Instinctively, I roll into him. He wraps me in his strong embrace, in his uniquely amazing smell, and I fall immediately to sleep.

I'M WOKEN BY BLARING ALARMS THAT HAVE ME bolting straight out of bed. I barely have time to notice that Kade is gone while searching for my sundress. After what feels like eternity, but is probably only a few seconds while multiple ear-piercing horn bursts ricochet through the tiny space, I locate it half-draped behind the dresser. The heels are thankfully easier to find and I grab my wristlet wallet and tumble out of the door just as the alarms stop.

Down the hall, a line of people appear to be filing through the door to the stairs for the main deck one level up.

The PA system crackles to life. "General emergency alarm test complete. Passengers, please make your way to your designated muster station."

Ah. That's right. The muster drill is this morning. Couldn't they have done this before departure like all the normal, commercial cruise lines do? But then, this isn't a commercial cruise. It's a high-end private cruise.

And as annoying as this is, it'll be ancient history soon and I'll be lying on a beach on a private island. Getting massages from hunky locals. Eating the best food of my life.

I decide I can make it through this one, tiny inconvenience.

So I trudge down the hall, running my fingers through my hair and hoping I don't look as trashed as I feel. Which is pretty damn trashed. My head is pounding, though that may have been all the noise. My hair is a tangled mess that my fingers are doing nothing to help. And I'm sure my makeup is smeared all to hell. Which goes with the odor of sex and alcohol nicely. I roll my eyes as I join the crowd at the stairs.

I'm able to avoid much notice until we're on the main deck, huddled in a large group, and a gaggle of older ladies start giving me knowing looks. I do my best to slink to the back of the pack while our assigned crew member goes over emergency procedures, but they continue to shoot me knowing and judgmental looks the whole time.

Joke's on them, because I don't regret last night for one minute. Best sex of my life with one of the hottest men I've ever seen? I don't even need to qualified that with "naked." Nope. No regrets.

Still.

I can't say I feel less jilted. Sure, I forgot about Kevin for one night. And had multiple, much-needed orgasms. But it's not exactly like I plan to do it again. Mostly because I feel like I've gotten it out of my system. Not exactly something I need to do on repeat to prove that I can. Besides, this ship isn't big enough to avoid being noticed if I do that every night. Nor is the resort. Which is why I picked it. A small, private romantic getaway.

Fuck romance. Fuck couples getaways. Fuck Kevin. Beach. Massages. Food.

I repeat the three words to myself like a mantra to calm myself and refocus on what I'm getting out of this. This will be relaxing. Fun. And then I'll go back to my normal life and start fresh, sans Kevin.

A DAY AND A HALF AND A MILD CASE OF BOREDOM later, we arrive at the private island. So tiny it doesn't even have a name. Just a modestly-sized resort with enough bungalows for the passengers of the small cruise to spend ten days in paradise.

The late August evening is bright and balmy as I disembark and climb into a vehicle not much bigger than a golf cart driven by a very quiet older gentleman that gives me a big smile. And when he drops me off fifteen minutes later, I give him a big tip. I'm living large now. I know this cruise is frequented by the rich, celebrities, and the like, so I don't want to get a reputation as the bad tipper. I can't imagine that would do much for my experience here.

I spend the evening having a leisurely room-service dinner, a long bubble bath, capped off with falling asleep reading a good book.

So when I wake the next morning, I'm in a damn good mood and ready to enjoy the spoils of my ruined relationship. Starting with a massage after a quick breakfast. Then a facial. Then a mani-pedi, because what the hell, that's what spas are for, right?

After lunch, I'm finally ready for some beach time. I make my way to the group of canopied loungers spread out at one end of the resort's beach only to find they're all taken. Guess that's what I get for waiting until the afternoon to get out here.

I keep walking and finally find a good spot of beach with a bit of shade from a nearby palm tree. I spread out my towel, slather my pale skin with sunscreen, and lay out on my tummy, book at the ready.

As I read, the calmness of my surroundings washes over me, undoing so much of the tension I've been holding these past weeks. I can hear the low buzz of conversation from the loungers a bit away, the gentle lapping of the crystal-blue waves at the shore, broken up by the occasional indignant squawk of a shore bird fighting over French fries from a carelessly discarded lunch tray. I smile sleepily as I try to focus on the book. But even though it's one of my favorite authors, the heat and relaxation are too great of a pull.

"DAKOTA."

I groggily open my eyes, unsure whether I heard the voice in my dreams or in real life. The tear of a page pulling away from my retreating sticky forehead tells me I fell asleep on my book. Oops.

I push myself onto my side to be met with a crouching Kade.

I spring up in shock. "Oh my god, Kade," I blurt out. Nope. Definitely not a dream.

He rises from his haunches with that damn sexy smirk looking like he wants to say something naughty. But instead, he says, "I didn't mean to startle you, but I saw you turning into a lobster, and I couldn't not wake you."

My brows bunch together at his comment as I dive for the cell phone in my bag. Shit. I've been asleep out here for more than two hours. I try to peer over my shoulder at the damage but I can't see much.

"How bad is it?" I ask, peering back up at him.

He offers a hand and helps me rise. "Nothing some aloe vera won't fix," he assures me.

I'm finally with it enough to take things in. The first thing I notice is that Kade is wearing a pair of fitted, white board shorts. And he's dripping wet.

"Know where I can get some?" I ask, finally finding my brain again. "All I brought was suntan lotion."

"Well, they probably have some at the resort," he replies slowly glancing back toward the low-slung building in the distance. "But I have some back in my room too."

His eyes flick back to mine, and I'm not sure exactly how far he meant that invitation to extend. But knowing my pale ass, I'm going to be in a lot of pain if I don't do something about it soon.

"Sure, that'd be great, thanks," I reply as noncha- lantly as possible. "I can drop by later when you'll be around."

"I'm around now," he responds. "No time like the present."

I snatch up my book, towel, and bag and gesture back toward the resort. "Lead the way then."

"So you're really here by yourself, then, huh?" he asks, glancing around like he expects some guy to pop out of the bushes and claim me.

I glance up at him warily.

"Should I be worried about being alone with you?" I try to sound like I'm teasing, but suddenly I remember how little I know this guy. Like not naked.

"I'd say that ship has sailed, wouldn't you?" he teases back. "Pun intended." He smiles widely and my punny ass falls just a little bit.

"Fair enough," I agree.

"Good. But you didn't answer the question."

I narrow my eyes and purse my lips at him. "Yes, I'm here alone."

He raises an eyebrow and faces forward, pointedly staying silent as he leads us on the stone path around the main building to the bungalows.

I sigh heavily. "I was supposed to be here with my fiancé." Kade's jaw drops and he turns to me, looking more than a little worried, so I rush to reassure him. "But I caught him cheating on me a month ago and we broke up. I figured no sense wasting a nice vacation."

Kade smiles sadly. "A non-refundable one, at that," he adds.

I laugh. "That too."

"So the rose petals …"

I squirm uncomfortably. "Yes. Apparently since a couple was booked into the room they gave me the 'romance package,'" I reply grumpily.

"Well, glad it didn't go to waste then."

"That wasn't romance, that was sex."

Kade stops and turns to face me, so close I can smell the ocean on his skin. Goosebumps pimple over my arms at his proximity.

"It was fucking fantastic sex," he corrects me. He gestures to the bungalow door I didn't realize we were standing next to. "Aloe vera?"

"Just aloe vera?" I ask, not giving away whether I want more or not.

Kade's bright blue eyes search mine. He leans forward, gently kissing me. My insides twist, but he pulls away before I can so much as react.

"No, Dakota. After the other night, it will never be just aloe vera."

I press my lips together to suppress the shit-eating grin that wants to break over my face and give an affected shrug.

"If you say so."

He snickers and unlocks the door, holding it open for me. I walk into a room nearly identical to the one I'm staying in, but for the men's clothes scattered about and the smell of him everywhere. I breathe in deeply before I can stop myself.

I whip my head around self-consciously, but thankfully Kade has disappeared into the bathroom. He reemerges a moment later with a giant bottle of green goo and a glint in his eye.

"Strip and lay down," he commands.

I stare at him for a moment while I decide how to play this. I'm only wearing a bikini, and it's not like he hasn't seen every inch of my naked body before. So I untie the string at my back and let the top fall to the floor. Then I slide the bottoms over my hips and let them join the top.

I allow Kade's eyes to rove hungrily over my curves for a moment before I turn and climb slowly onto the bed, laying gently on my stomach and pulling my hair over my shoulder.

I'd like to say I'm the kind of sex vixen that could do it confidently, but nerves twist at my tummy wondering if he'll find me as attractive in the bright light of day.

But when his weight sinks onto the bed and cold, slippery hands meet my back, all of my cares fly out the window. So we're doing this. A vacation fling. I can get on board with that.

And I can definitely get on board with the slow, strong strokes of his hands massaging the cooling lotion into my heated back. Thankfully I don't seem to have burned too badly, but he's right, aloe vera is exactly what I needed.

Then, he shifts to straddling me so he can reach my other side and I feel his bare cock on my ass.

"Kade, are you naked?" I gasp in surprise.

A low chuckle meets my ears as his hands mirror strokes down my sides. "Took you long enough."

I wiggle my ass teasingly into his cock and his hands stop. Then withdraw. Then I feel them land on the backs of my legs, abruptly pushing them forward, launching my backside into the air.

"What are you —" But when his face meets my folds, I'm rendered speechless. "Ohhhh." The moan slips out before I can stop it.

His tongue fucks me like he means it, alternating spearing into me and flicking hard against my clit. It's enough to drive me wild without taking me all the way.

"You like that?" he asks, his voice humming through me.

"I'd like your cock in me even more," I return sassily.

"Goddamn, Dakota." I hear the rip of foil, a dip of the bed, then he slams into me. And doesn't stop. The sunburnt backs of my legs sting every time his body meets mine, adding a slight pain to the intense pleasure that somehow makes it even more heady.

This time he doesn't stop me from just taking it, not that I could do much else right now. It feels too damn good and soon I'm coming all over his cock, screaming his name like I've never screamed anyone's name before.

I make to sink down, but Kade's hands catch my hips, hauling me upright. He turns around me, lays down, and pulls me over him.

"You don't want to lay on that back," he warns me.

"You're right," I agree, sliding onto him. "I want to ride you until you're screaming *my* name." I slam down, and this time I'm the one who doesn't stop. I buck and twist and fuck him within an inch of his life, until he goes slack and is moaning under me.

I lean forward, gripping his pecs and letting my hips swing freely. It forces his cock into my G-spot, and I tighten hard around him.

"Holy shit," he gasps. "That … oh my god, that …" And with that, he roars my name as he comes. The pulsing of his cock pushes me over the edge with him and stars burst in my vision.

I slump onto his chest, breathing hard. His hands come to rest on my ass, the only part of my backside that's *not* burned.

"See. I say so," he says simply, and it takes me a minute to remember that he means it will never be just aloe vera.

I laugh so hard, it pushes him out of me. With an answering grin, he shifts me off of him, removes the condom, and discards it in a tissue.

I sink back into the bed, lying on my stomach, and Kade settles on his back next to me.

"What's your last name, Dakota?" he asks thoughtfully.

I smile. "Mitchell. You?"

He turns and gives me a puzzled look.

"What?"

He shakes his head. "Nothing. It's Ryan."

I laugh. "Kade Ryan?" I giggle harder after saying it out loud.

"You think my name's funny?"

That makes me laugh even harder. "Uhh … yeah, I guess I do. Sounds like a porn star." The words pop out before I can stop them, and I flush with embarrassment. But then again, he is ridiculously good in bed. I give him a look of horror. "Oh god, you're not a porn star, are you?"

Now it's Kade's turn to laugh. "No, I'm not a porn star."

I prop myself up on an elbow. "So what are you? I mean, what do you do for a living?"

He shrugs. "A little bit of this. A little bit of that."

I frown, but I can't exactly give him crap for dodging the question. It's not like this is more than sex, so he doesn't owe me anything.

"Do you sell Band-Aids?" I ask suddenly.

Kade scoffs. "No. What gave you that idea?"

I roll my lips through my teeth. "You … smell like them?"

Kade bursts into laughter. Like, rolling around holding his stomach kind of laughter.

I curl up into a self-conscious ball, tucking my head into my knees. I feel him pull at my legs, then slide up flush against me. His finger tugs my chin up and our eyes meet.

"That is the cutest fucking thing I've ever heard," he says before planting the steamiest kiss on me. Like, the slow, languid, toe-curling kind of kiss a girl dreams about.

"Mmm. I should say stupid things like that more if that's what I get for it," I murmur against his lips.

He pulls back and looks at me. "This is all backwards, I know, but will you have dinner with me?"

I cock my head to the side. "Really?"

He kisses my nose and smiles. "Really. The more I talk to you, the more I like you."

"Oh. Well … same, actually. So yes. You mean like … now?" I clarify.

Kade laughs. "Yes. I mean like now. If that's cool."

"That's very cool. I'm flattered, actually."

"I'm the one that's flattered. You're different, Dakota. Than other women. It's refreshing."

I give him an incredulous look. "It's refreshing that a woman is good for more than just sex?"

Kade's lips dip into an uncharacteristic frown. "It's refreshing that a woman is interested in me for … more than just sex."

Something inside me twinges. "Oh, Kade. I'm sorry. I didn't … I mean, yes, this was about sex. But if we'd met anywhere else, I'm pretty sure this would've gone the more normal way. You know, getting to know each other first, then mind-blowing sex," I assure him.

"I'm not sure I even know what the 'normal way' is," he admits. "And I sure as hell don't regret the mind-blowing sex coming first —"

"Pun intended?" I interrupt teasingly.

Kade chuckles. "Let's go get something to eat, yeah?"

I chew at my lip. Is this really happening? Does this

gorgeous, sweet, sexy man really want to take me on a date?

"Yeah."

AFTER WHAT WAS UNDOUBTEDLY THE BEST NIGHT OF MY life, I get back to my bungalow mid-morning and hit the shower. I'd love to spend all day smelling like Kade, but after our nonstop sex-fest, a shower is a must.

The next thing I do is pick up my phone to call my best friend so I can gush about not only the amazing sex I've been having, but about our date. I pause, phone in hand, and I'm sure stars in my eyes as I remember how we spent almost as long talking as we did fucking. How funny he is. How alike we are in our interests and values. Which is an interesting thing to discuss with someone you thought was a one-night stand, but there it is. And miraculously, it turns out we both live in the same city. Which I guess isn't that miraculous as it's the major metropolitan area the cruise departed from. But still. This could be … something. Maybe.

Shaking myself from memories, I punch in my passcode and open to my home screen. Only to see I've got a text from said best friend.

Dakota! I'm shocked and proud! Get it, girl! A link follows her declaration. My brows scrunch together and I click the link, wondering what she could possibly be talking about.

The page to some gossip site loads and my hand flies to my mouth as a gasp escapes me.

Cruising for Love! Kade "The Killer" Ryan, 33, seen frolicking on the beach with mysterious blonde beauty.

It seems our favorite hunky, notorious playboy UFC light heavyweight champion has been using the downtime between fights to woo an unknown woman on a private beach cruise to…
Click for more

Below the headline and teaser is a picture. Of Kade and I. Kissing in front of his bungalow. My lobster-red half-covered ass on full display. With the distinctive tattoo on my hip showing. Splashed all over the internet.

"No no no no no no no," I moan. How utterly humiliating. Kade is … famous? Well, that sure explains his reticence to talk about his work. Oh my god. I'm fucking a famous guy and my ass is all over the internet. The trolls are going to tear me to absolute shreds. Oh no. No no no. This is not good. This has to stop.

I pace the floor as I try to decide what to do. I'm supposed to meet Kade at his cabin this evening again for dinner and … well, ya know, probably more.

I'll just stay here.

But then he'll come looking for me.

I'll switch cabins.

It's a private fucking island, dipshit, he'll find you.

Or will he?

I have his number now. I could not be a chicken and just text him the link and let him know I'm out.

God, I can't do that.

This. This is why he said women only want him for sex. Except he meant sex and fame, he just didn't want to say it. So here I am, a woman who wanted him for him, and I'd be rejecting him too.

God, I can't do that.

Before I can stop myself, my fingers are flying over the phone.

I'm freaking out over here. I need to talk.

I hit send and fling my phone down on the bed, not really expecting an immediate answer. But still, I wait for one, chewing my fingernails and staring the phone down like it's an angry spider that might jump on me at any moment.

I'm startled out of my anxiety by a knock on the door and open it to find Kade.

"Hey." His tone is subdued though he's as gorgeous as ever, a dark lock dipping into his eyes, day-old stubble making him look perfectly imperfect.

My mouth opens and closes repeatedly, I'm sure making me look like a fish. I just don't know what to say.

"Hi?"

"Are you gonna let me in?" he asks tentatively as I peep around the barely opened door at him.

I step back, shaking my head. "Sorry, yes, of course."

He steps inside, nervously shoving his hands in the pockets of his board shorts. Thankfully he's wearing a white tank, so he's ever so slightly less distracting than he would be without it.

"So I saw the gossip this morning," he leads.

I nod and sink onto the end of the bed, still in shock.

"I assume that's what you wanted to talk about?" he asks softly, settling next to me.

I nod again, this time in shock that it was him I messaged instead of … well, anyone else.

"Why didn't you tell me?" I whisper.

"You really can't guess?"

"I *could*, or you could just give it to me straight."

He blows a sharp breath out his nose. "I liked that you didn't know who I was. I mean, I don't know when I was going to tell you … if I was going to. And I certainly didn't want you to find out like that. I just … I guess I wanted to see if this was … something."

I close my eyes and sigh, tears stinging the backs of my eyelids. I always get emotional when I'm nervous. "I get that," I admit, opening my eyes to find him looking worriedly at me. "And I really like you, Kade. Last night was the best date I've ever had but —"

He holds up a hand. "Does there have to be a but?"

I huff a small laugh. "I … wish there didn't. Because …" I stare at him. God, I really do *like* this guy. It may have started as hot sex, and it may end as just hot sex … but is it really fair that we don't get to figure out for ourselves whether there's more here? "I just went through the wringer with my ex."

Kade smirks. "I'm cool being your rebound guy, Dakota. I'll be whatever guy you want if you're willing to give this a shot."

My heart simultaneously melts and breaks. "I'm not cool using you, though … I think I could. Give this a shot. But we're still on vacation and the paparazzi already have pictures of my ass all over the internet. I'm not sure I could handle the level of scrutiny I smell coming, Kade."

He scrubs his hands down his face, over his budding beard. "That's fair. But there are ways to do this under the radar, you know."

I look at him skeptically. "Because clearly that's been working so well?"

His lips thin into a tight line. "And my manager is working on that. I went on this cruise specifically so I didn't have to worry about that. They were supposed to be taking measures. Apparently instead they were taking bribes. But I've been doing this a long time. And yes, we can do this without that kind of attention all the time."

"But sometimes?" I press.

Kade looks at me wearily. "Yes. Sometimes." He rises abruptly from the bed and stalks to the door frame, landing a punch. "Fuck, I just once want this to not be an issue." He shakes out his hand.

"Hey, don't take it out on my doorframe, okay?" I tease, rising and grabbing his hand, running my thumb over his knuckles.

He smirks, but this time there's no heat in it. Just disappointment. "Don't worry, I know how to pull my punches."

I huff a laugh. "I'll bet."

That gets a smile out of him. "I like you, Dakota."

He draws closer, pulling me into his embrace.

I look up at him, just as entranced as the first time. "I like you too, Kade."

A spark lights in his gaze. He leans in, brushing his lips against mine. Lightly at first, then more deeply. Kissing me like he means it. Like he's playing for keeps. Or at least hoping to try.

"Will you trust me enough to let me show you? That we can do this quietly. Just long enough to see if this is really what I think it could be."

I look at him in disbelief. "You seem awfully …"

"Intense? Yeah. I guess I am. But I wasn't kidding, Dakota. This doesn't happen to me. Sex doesn't turn into finding out the woman who rocked your world is also funny and easy to talk to. That is someone you can't wait to see again. Someone who makes you want to deal with all the subterfuge bullshit just to get a chance to know her."

There's that damn swoon again. And this time it isn't his body making me swoon. It's his heart.

I decide he may have a point. It might just work out. And isn't that worth a shot?

"No more kissing outside with my ass on display."

His brows jump. "Is that a yes?"

"That's a yes."

Kade kisses me hard, pushing me back toward the bed. We tumble down, with me laughing underneath him as he peppers me with kisses everywhere he can reach. "Agreed. All kissing will be done right here. Or in my bed. Fuck, right here. Because we may never leave," he murmurs as his hands slip under my skirt.

I thread my fingers into his thick, dark hair as he works his magic on my body. "Oh but we will," I sigh.

His head snaps up and I smile down at him.

"I mean, we have to get back on the cruise ship in a week. So you know. We'll have to switch beds eventually."

Kade laughs and crawls up my body, trapping me under him and kissing me roughly.

"You had me going for a minute there," he says.

I grin and kiss him. "That *was* awfully mean. I think I deserve a spanking."

He sucks in a sharp breath. "Damn, Dakota, it's like you're reading my mind." He wraps his arms around me and rolls so I'm on top of him, then smacks my backside playfully. "This ass is mine."

I straddle him and grind into his cock. "Only if you treat it right."

Kade's grin drops and he pulls me toward him. "I may have a rep, Dakota, but I don't cheat, and I know how to treat a woman like a fucking queen. You don't have to take my word for it though. I'll show you."

I put my hands on his face, stroking my thumbs over his cheeks. "I believe you. And you should know you could never be just a rebound guy, Kade." I don't say more. I can't. Because I'm pretty sure Kade is right. That there's something here.

Because I don't feel any of the hurt and anger anymore. Only the hope. And hope feels a lot like the beginning of something very special. Something a lot like love.

Want more? Check out Melanie A. Smith's latest release *Finding His Redemption: An Enemies to Lovers Rock Star Romance* at https://melanieasmithauthor. com/books-finding-his-redemption.html

Sign up for Melanie A. Smith's newsletter to get a FREE book plus all the latest news and more https://mailchi.mp/melanieasmithauthor.com/nlsignup

A NOTE FROM THE AUTHOR

Thank you so much for reading! Now … I need your help! Will you please take a minute to leave a review? It doesn't have to be long — just a couple sentences saying what you thought of the book on any retailer, goodreads, and/or BookBub. Your opinion is important to me, and for potential readers. Thank you!

ABOUT THE AUTHOR

Melanie A. Smith is an award-winning and international best-selling author of steamy contemporary romance fiction. A voracious reader and lifelong writer, Melanie's writing began at a young age with short stories and poetry. After college and a career as an aircraft engineer, she shifted to domestic engineering and property management and eventually found a balance where she was able to return to writing fiction. Melanie is also a Mensan and enjoys spending time with her family, cooking, and driving with the windows down and the stereo cranked up loud.

facebook.com/MelanieASmithAuthor
twitter.com/MelASmithAuthor
instagram.com/melanieasmithauthor